DINOSAUR MAZES

RICH LATTA

PRICE STERN SLOAN

Los Angeles

Copyright © 1990 by Rich Latta
Illustrations © 1990 by Price Stern Sloan, Inc.
Published by Price Stern Sloan, Inc.
11150 Olympic Boulevard, Suite 650, Los Angeles, California 90064

ISBN: 0-8431-2822-4
10 9 8 7 6 5 4 3

STEGOSAURUS
(STEG-uh-sor-us)

IGUANODON
(ih-GWAN-uh-don)

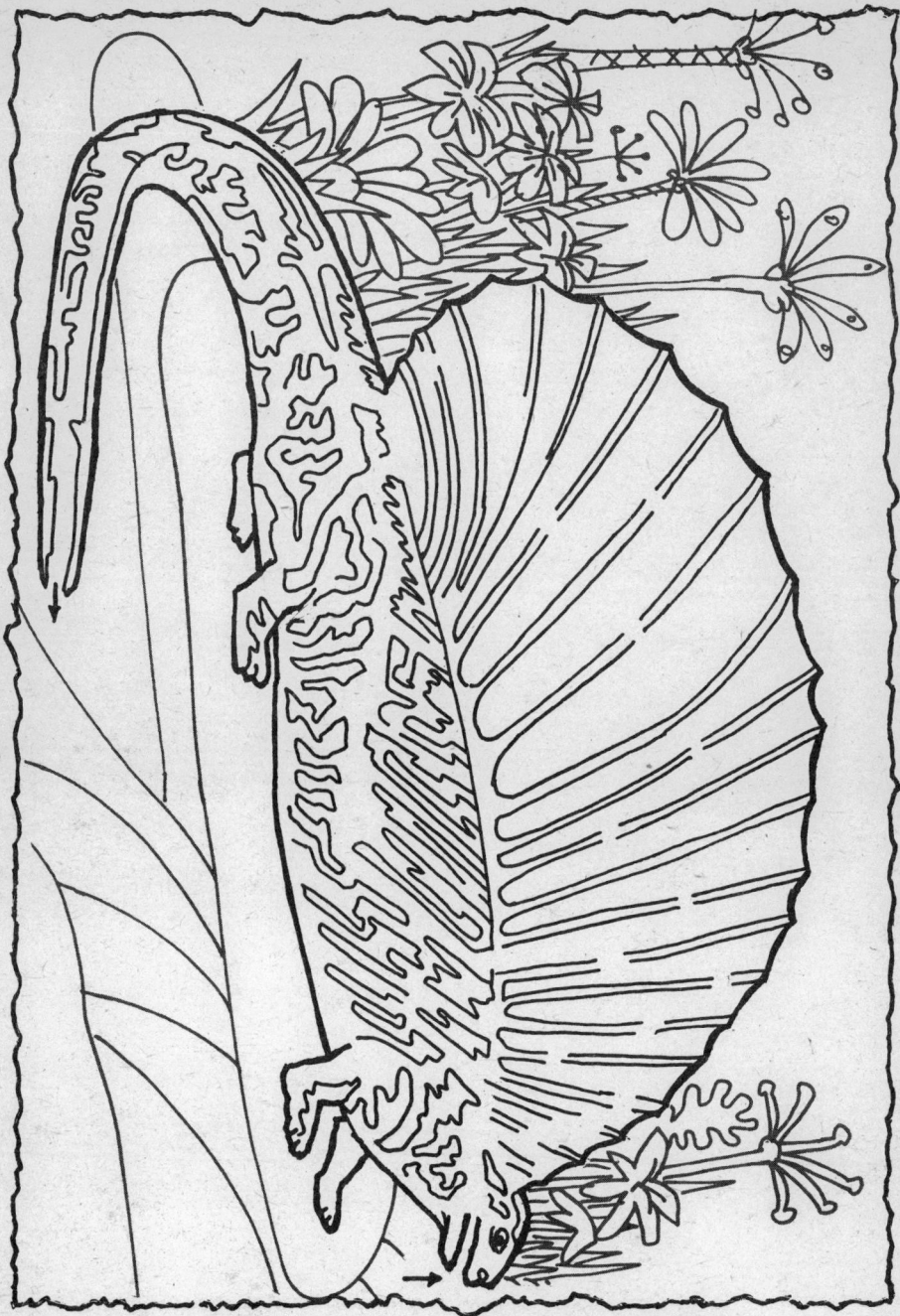

EDAPHOSAURUS
(e-DAF-uh-sor-us)

ORNITHOLESTES
(or-nith-o-LESS-teez)

PTERANODON
(tair-AN-o-don)

TRICERATOPS
(try-SAIR-uh-tops)

ANKYLOSAURUS

(an-KILE-uh-sor-us)

TYRANNOSAURUS
(tie-RAN-uh-sor-us)

PARASAUROLOPHUS
(par-au-sor-OL-uh-fus)

STYRACOSAURUS
(sty-RAK-uh-sor-us)

DIMETRODON
(dye-MET-ruh-don)

TRACHODON
(TRAK-uh-don)

RHAMPHORHYNCHUS
(ram-fo-RINK-us)

BRACHIOSAURUS
(brayk-ee-uh-SOR-us)

PACHYCEPHALOSAURUS
(pak-ee-SEF-uh-lo-sor-us)

ELASMOSAURUS

(ee-LAZ-muh-sor-us)

DIPLODOCUS
(dih-PLOD-uh-kus)

ARCHAEOPTERYX
(ar-kee-OP-ter-ix)

PROTOCERATOPS
(pro-toe-SAIR-uh-tops)

APATOSAURUS
(ah-PAT-uh-sor-us)

ALLOSAURUS
(AL-uh-sor-us)

LAMBEOSAURUS
(LAM-be-uh-sor-us)

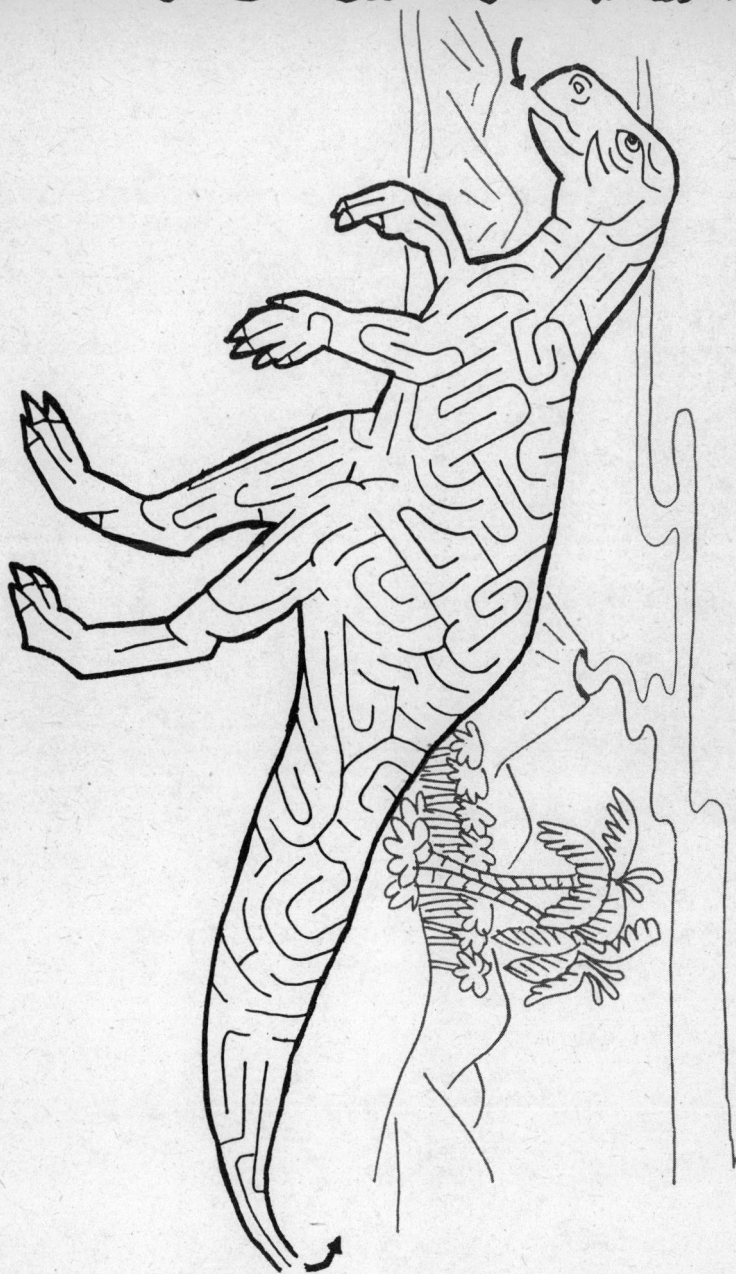

DRYOSAURUS
(dry-uh-SOR-us)